This book is dedicated to the following:

Michael Linarello
Daryl Tomkins
Emma Zurcher-Long
Gary J. Kucich
Wendi & Benjamin Dial
Stephen Caraccia

The Quiet Bear

By Gretchen Leary
Illustrated By Melissa Saylor

There once was a very little girl whose voice matched her tiny size.

She lived in a quiet little town that, like the girl, hardly ever spoke a word.

One day the little girl and her family packed their belongings and moved to the city.

The loud buildings loomed like mountains and the crowds marched on like drums.

When autumn came, the little girl and her family went to the park for the afternoon.

As they walked through the park, they passed a tattered old bear sitting on a bench.

The little girl and the bear sat together quietly as the busy city swirled and hummed about, like the leaves that fell around them.

Without a word, the bear told her all about the glitter and glamour of city life.

As the sun began to set, the little girl took the quiet bear by the hand to head on home.

They sat quietly together on the crowded subway as it rattled along the rails.

They sat quietly in the taxi as it wove in and out around the crowded city.

At dinner the bear wasn't very hungry.

He seemed too full of stories to share.

When it was time for bed, the little girl said "Goodnight my friend."

And though she spoke without a sound, the bear heard every word.

The End

Acknowledgements

Troy Jordan
Suzanne Edwards
Sandra A. Madden
Mckenzie Edwards
Jeanne Webb
Sara Vinas
Todd Civin
Leah Kelley
Camille Detrick
Anna Tucker
Joseph Caraccia
Nolan Kucich
Hayley Kucich
Traci Stewart